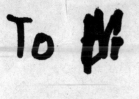

Restrict

a poetic narrative

Sol Rivera

hatherleigh

RESTRICT

Text Copyright © 2023 Sol Rivera

Library of Congress Cataloging-in-Publication Data is available.
ISBN: 978-1-57826-984-6

Cover and Interior Design by Carolyn Kasper
Author Photography by Kim Ponsky

Printed in the United States
10 9 8 7 6 5 4 3 2 1

For everyone who encouraged
me to write from the heart.

Contents

Author's Note

IT HAS BEEN ALMOST a year since I conceived the idea for Restrict, which was at the dawn of my transition into teenhood. A rocky period leading up through middle school to the end of ninth grade had ended. Still reeling from its aftermath, I was on one of those quarantine walks that scientists continue to recommend when it dawned on me—that I had relatable childhood experiences of struggling with an eating disorder. I knew I had to write something, a letter to my past self that others could read as well. When I started to write this story, I felt as though it was far-fetched.

However, through the cathartic poetry writing process, I have heard from others who have experienced pre-adolescent disordered eating. Most of my peers have struggled with insecurity in some way, and sadly we live in a world where it often has to do with something as beautiful and sacred as our bodies. The way Restrict sits with me is the way

I hope everyone who reads this poetic narrative can consciously come to terms with their own insecurities. I know with all my heart that if I could repeat everything, I would tell my own little girl self from a decade ago that her body is not a competition to be won. I have to remind myself of that in the present as well. Thank you for reading, and I hope that we tell all of our little girls inside of us that we do not have to be perfect to be loved.

Where We Are

A girl
Who runs and plays
And doesn't think about calories
Or her intake of them

She hears whispers
Of Mother complaining about gaining weight
About a new diet her friend wants her to try
How they'll both be skinny

Whispers spread
But when she enters the room
They disappear
Little girls shouldn't be worried
About weight after all

But children are curious
And so Little Girl with a cupcake and a remote
Turns on the TV
And sees some no name real housewife
Pedaling protein powder
Exercise routines
Weight Watchers

Saying to all the other little girls
That skinny is normal, pretty
Signs of status
(You are anything but)

Little Girl takes her cupcake

Throws it away
(This is where it starts)

We're Just Children
After All

The seed had been planted
But it was a dry spring
There was no place
For it to grow

Unfortunately, it seems
Little Girl is entering a rainforest
A school full of other little girls
With hundreds of seeds
Waiting to grow
Some, sprouting
Others, fully formed

One of these fully formed plants
Looking similar to a catalog model
With a hot pink backpack and shoes to match
Comes up to the Little Girl
And pours poisoned water
On her waiting seed of self-doubt
Asks her to play a game

Girls are like games
Some are boring
Some draw you in
A parasitic relationship
That falls apart
When there is nothing left in the end

But, sweet, sorta confident Little Girl
Doesn't know the kinds of games other girls play
So when Miss Hot Pink comes up to her
She says yes

The First Game

The game is easy enough
There aren't many rules
Only two things needed
A scale
And a secret room

Miss Hot Pink explained
That the winner was the one who weighed less
And got nothing
But pleasure

Little Girl understood
For the first time
That less is better
And skinny is a compliment
Not just an adjective
(They just learned what those are in class; her
    favorite one was light)

So they played their little game
In Little Girl's mother's bathroom
(Not at Hot Pink's, never at Hot Pink's)
Hot Pink would always win

70 pounds on the dot
While Little Girl was 88.78
Which was a less pretty number

According to the two of them

They played this game over and over
And found out that they could
Play against themselves
88.79 could be 87.2 the next day
And wasn't that spectacular?

And yet it was only a number
(They hadn't had Instagram yet, after all—didn't
    know of flat stomachs or clear skin or *thinspo*)
Still, they avoided
Cupcakes after that
Even if the nanny made them fresh
On Sundays

Rebecca

The nanny had stopped making cupcakes
   on Sundays
But that was okay
(Even if it wasn't)
Little Girl wouldn't touch them

Second grade would be different
Miss Hot Pink was in another class
So there was a lifesaver
Rebecca

Rebecca was proud
Of herself
Of what she would do
Not fake proud like Miss Hot Pink
But self-assured

Loud

Although Miss Hot Pink would notice
And the Little Girl and her carpooled every day
So they would gossip

About Rebecca
The only one who saw Little Girl for what she was

Lost

Hot Pink would whisper
She's ugly, poor too
(Poor for them meant two-bedroom apartments
Not the homeless they were driven past in 100,000
    dollar SUVs)
And Little Girl would think
Not at all
But would agree anyway

The guilt was insurmountable
So Little Girl who was told from the start
That she could do no wrong
And that everyone will love her
Told Rebecca
Everything

The lies and the rumors
The stories about her darker skin
How Miss Hot Pink said the n word once

Rebecca and Little Girl
Weren't friends
After that

But Miss Hot Pink and Little Girl had a sleepover
So it all worked out
Right?

Sleepaway Camp

Are you tired of raising your children?
Four nannies not enough?
Can your pre-teen play tennis?
Lucky for you!
A once in a lifetime opportunity
Is on its way

It's called sleepaway camp
And for the low price of seven grand a month
Your second grader can go, too!

First, we'll put 13 girls in a cabin
All taught to be obsessed with their looks
Then we sprinkle in two 17-year-olds
Who like drinking more than children
Lastly, a treat—no Wi-Fi
And you're shamed for reading
Because God forbid you want peace
After 15 hours of activity

Mother thinks this sounds splendid
(The Hamptons won't drink itself, you know)
And so Little Girl is there on day one

Crying on day two
And kissing a boy on day three

But she picks up another habit

Because things have been good for too long
So she compares her meals to other girls
Just as little and scared as
she
Notices their portions
Cuts her own in half
Her shirts are too big two weeks in
(She likes the feeling of being loose)

Two months later
She's happy, skinny
Maybe even weighs less than Miss Hot Pink
But her mom notices
And she's put on an I.V.
Commanded never to go to camp
Again
(Except she will every year thereafter)

An interlude: little girls

The thing they don't tell you about little girls
Is that they can be twice as vicious as the media
   tells them to be
Using tips and tricks
To get them to the top

The pyramid of social success still exists
Especially when there is nothing else to measure
Like followers or wealth
They haven't learned that
Not yet

Hottest commodity?
Their bodies
How many they can attract with it

Because they don't have much else
(Not even when they grow up to be adults)

Little boys will notice them
Give them what they crave
Attention

And the feeling of being pretty
That will go away once day turns to night
And another little girl goes on her way

They're taught that little boys are what turns little
    girls into *real women*
(Little boys are only taught what we tell them)
They aren't gods
They *are* two inches taller
And for a third grader
That's enough

The Second Game

There's a game going around
(Girls love their games)
And the characters correspond
To your standing

The kicker?
There's only 13 players
And those who aren't invited
Are cast to the sidelines
To play jump rope
Or whatever

Even if you are a player
Like Little Girl is

You still have to be the ranking that fits you best

13 girls
Little Girl is in the top two
Miss Hot Pink is number one

There's Naturally Skinny
And East Coast Barbie
Also another girl
Odette
Last on the list
Who everyone (even Rebecca) thinks strange

Odette carries herself oddly
With clothes that came from thrift stores
And a mother who was an academic
Instead of a philanthropist
She didn't even have an iPad or an email
The horror

Little Girl learned to be mean
To ridicule others who weren't the same
Naturally Skinny invited her to her penthouse
And they knew what they were doing was wrong
Yet they gossiped about Oddette
And laughed quietly when the teacher called her
    out in class

Her mom was mad
Like any good mother would be
But Little Girl's and Naturally Skinny's fathers
   were donors to the school
(12 million between the two of them)
So the principal said that girls exaggerate
And left the poor mother alone

Her daughter's pride ruined

So the girls in the school heard
And were taught another lesson that day
Taught that parents were important
And that the threat of punishments
Was shit
If you could pay

Millionaire Status

Summer before Third Grade
Little Girl learns two things:

1)
A fundraiser was taking place in the living room
Adults only
Nine-year-olds not allowed
Her nanny
Tucked her in

The tucking in stopped
And Little Girl learned her first thing that summer
"You know, Little Girl
Your parents are millionaires
Not only that
Multimillionaires
The kind of wealth that rivals celebrities
The kind that brings in sycophants and servants"
(Not that Little Girl knows what those are)

Millionaire meant a lot, she knew

But for all she thought
It was only something to brag about
Something new

Summer ended
Camp and the Hamptons
What else?

2)
When summer ended
School began
And lunch became an interview
Of how nice your vacations were
Little Girl blurts out what she soon regrets

"You know, my parents are millionaires
Not only that, *multi-millionaires*"
The other girls laughed
Little Girl, they say, in between cackles
We're all millionaires
You're nothing special

Little Girl learned that day
Of course those things wouldn't matter
She could never be enough
But she could be *less*
(Lesser is better and your status isn't shit)

Resurgence

It's been a year and five months
Little Girl has been distracted
By games and humiliation
It's time to start again

She wasn't very successful last time
Whatever weight she lost
She gained back

All it would take was a new perspective
A new lease on life
(Not really)

Little Girl knows
That you lose weight without eating
But there's another way
Messier but better

She googles How To Throw Up
(The idea comes because you can skip school
    if you do)
And she practices so much
She can't see food without gagging

One day she is by herself
Laying down in a pile of vomit
And yet Little Girl laughs up a storm

Funny, isn't it?
That I ended up eating less
After all

Floors don't acknowledge tears

Birthdays

Mother says
There are three times when calories don't count

Vacations
Funerals
And
Birthdays

Lucky for Little Girl
She's 10 today
Double Digits
Her entire life ahead of her

She doesn't like that statement
Her entire life ahead of her
Didn't she have the future
Yesterday?

No, she didn't
Because she doesn't know what futures are yet
How they weave together
There are a million futures
A couple lead to good endings
The rest end up in utter despair

21

At least her despair
Will be another girl's dream
But she doesn't think of that

She thinks of cakes and cookies
Stuff she hasn't eaten for forever
Stuffing herself
Feeling guilty afterwards

Not enough
To stop celebrating
(It's a good birthday in her books)

An interlude:
mothers

Mothers were little girls once
Bright eyed
Innocent

They grew up with 70's sequoia furniture
   80's hairdos
90's technology
Three channels on the TV
All promoting whatever they could

They were the model generation
Of Kate Moss and Heroine Chic
Seeing first-hand
That size zero
Was the norm
(You are not that way = you are not the way
   that we want)

Their mothers were on diet pills
Before the knowledge that they caused cancer
Powders, supplements
All with FDA approval

Mothers were taught
No-nonsense knowledge
Their mothers taught them
The thing about knowledge?
It gets passed down through generations

(Little girls are screwed)

Visitas con Papa

After months of legal fees and arguments
It was decided
Little Girl was to go on a chartered plane
Twice a year to Puerto Rico
To visit her Dad

She treated this with the same annoyance
One has when their Wi-Fi goes down
Puerto Rico is not the worst place ever
But her Dad was
Something else

Mother is constant
She nitpicks on the little things
Bakes for the homeless
And focuses on herself

She treats Little Girl like
An ugly younger sister or a lady in waiting
With affection that carries the knowledge
That you will never be as good as me

Dad
(Papa, as he preferred)
Is in a state of flux
Remarried to a wife a couple years younger
Prettier (in the Post's opinion)
Who is bright and bubbly
Who had a daughter of her own
Who now has two fathers

Little Girl learns what it's like to be an outsider
On every visit

When jokes are made in familial bliss
And she's kept out of it all unintentionally

The not-so-new wife
(She and Dad have been married five years)
Reaches out to her, loves her
As one would any family member
They see twice a year

Little Girl is scared and jealous and mad every
    time she visits
Scared of Mother's rants when she comes back
Jealous of her half-sister's security at home
Most of all mad

Mad that Dad is the better parent
Who gives her gifts and smiles at her
   achievements
Not caring about appearances
Or calories on cardboard boxes

Mad that the judge agreed with Mother
Because she is a mother
And not for being *motherly* in any particular way

Mad that all she wants is her parents' full love
That doesn't have to be divided between
   two families
But all she has is a gray hole where a heart
   should go
And nothing to put in it

Dance Dance Revolution

The hottest dances of the year
$10,000 dollars for admittance
Middle Schoolers everywhere want a ticket

And Little Girl has a +1

Co-ed cohabitation
A first for many
No excuses to stay in a corner
Now it's time to chase boy's numbers

Miss Hot Pink (a +1)
An expert from her older sister
Knows what to do:

Say hello
Compliment them
Turn around and leave
They'll be begging for more
And soon you'll be drowning in their DMs

Little Girl has a first kiss
And a first weirdo
(Crop tops on teens shouldn't be inviting to men
    thirty years out of college)
But never a first boyfriend
She wonders what that's like

To know you are never alone
To have someone to sleep in your bed at night
And comfort you when you dream of
    ~~Mothers~~ monsters

So she stands with the rest of the girls
Too embarrassed to dance
While she gets three numbers
And texts none of them back

Logan

Well, that's not *exactly* true
One of them
Got her number from Miss Hot Pink
And sends her a *hey*

She responds
Starts to crave the attention he gives
The way he calls her beautiful
And looks more athletic than most guys she knows

Most of all she likes the confidence it gives her
Miss Hot Pink isn't dating anyone
And she thinks that must make herself special
Even Mother is proud

They meet up a couple times
They kiss and she says it's her first
She knows how much guys like that
To be the winner of a girl's purity

He holds her a bit closer
Says goodbye
And he asks for nudes the next day

Little Girl says *nope*
Bad things happen to girls who do
(She doesn't even have boobs to send)
He blocks her
And Little Girl binges when she finds out

Two weeks later
East Coast Barbie's nudes are leaked
And she doesn't show up to school

After that

An interlude:
diet soda

It isn't much
12 ounces a can
Sweet, syrupy
Zero calories

Made in a lab
Said to cause cancer
But no one cares
When they're drinking it by the gallon

In every restaurant
Said to be healthy
No one's gained weight from it
No one's tried

The last supper of many
When your brain won't let you eat
But your stomach growls
Held hostage
Hungry

It goes into your stomach
A river of chemicals
Mother buys more but she doesn't know why

But when it gets too much
The river starts flooding
It comes up the other direction
And feels like misery

So you crack open another can
And relish the sickness of skinny
There will be many more cans
But will never satisfy you enough

You crave the taste of nothing
To satiate your humanity
Be unreal

Bat Mitzvah

A phenomenon in NYC
Where Jewish American Princesses unite
For a religious ceremony
(Though the party is what makes or breaks it)

Well it's a big deal
For some who like that sort of thing
But Little Girl does not like parties

So Mother tells her to put on a bright face
There's one every week, you know
Make connections
(Make some new friends)

Logan sees her at one of them
He calls her a Little Slut
When she tells Miss Hot Pink
With a cracking voice, she laughs

There is a moment when everyone thinks
I need someone to love me right now

It is every moment
Every breath from the second we rise
To when we crash into our beds

It is the moment where we are selfish
But it's okay
Because love is worth being selfish for

It has conquered a million men
And a million women
But knowing this is meaningless

Because
Little Girl is in a ballroom bathroom
Mascara streaming down her face
Thinking
I need someone to love me right now
(The love never comes)

Karma Doesn't Care
If You're Insecure

What goes around
Comes around
And in Middle School
It isn't any different

You see
When gossipers gossip
They in turn are gossiped about
Little Girl has that lesson to learn
And it won't be pretty finding that out

When toxic backstabbing friends

Turn their knives on you
Suddenly there is no place
To run
Without blood

Little Girl is called a bully
For shame! For shame!
She takes to hiding in the bathroom
You know what she's doing
For shame! For shame!

36

Mother says to apologize
Little Girl agrees
So she flung herself at
Her 'best friend's' feet
The name? Miss Hot Pink

Oh brother
Let's hope karma's
A bitch

Restrict

Little Girl is back at her table
Her spot once again
Secure

But that youthful
Well, not innocence
(Willfulness)
Is ruined for good

She becomes enamored

With a certain kind of sadness
Where doubt festers
And nothingness pervades

Humans crave feeling
Little Girl is no different
But her body has taken a sabbatical
And instead of feeling?
Numbness

This is an inescapable prison
Chains hold her down

Telling her that she'll never be enough
(Never become less)
She craves the ability to feel
And sticks her finger down her throat

And in that pile of vomit
Sitting on the whitewashed floor
Lays Little Girl, praying
That someone feeling for her will come
She passes out soon after that
(At least in sleep there is no expectation of
    feeling at all)

Paris Syndrome

Even distant mothers see their children
Know they shouldn't have
Long glassy stares
Or yellow, rotting teeth that smell of stink

A trip would do Little Girl some good

To Paris, a city of love and light
A city that has its own mental illness attached to it.
(How fitting)

Little Girl allows herself to go
To be swung around the city
Like she was a child
And her mother was not a frigid bitch

So they visit the Louvre
Posted envy-racking pictures on Instagram
(Little Girl has 2,087 followers; she checks hourly)

But when they are at a boulangerie
Or a mouth-watering creperie
Mother looks down at her companion's plate
And *doesn't see her eat a thing*

Confusion is Key

Ninth Grade is when Little Girl Finds her purpose
Her challenge
(And maybe her college essay)

It's because of English class
And some judgmental kids

There's a short story
Little Girl clutches at
With long arms
That could be snapped
Like a twig

They read it last night
Little Girl was enraptured
By how much the girl in the story
Was like her

Never before was there a story more relatable
Actions most similar to hers
The lying, the eating
And the subsequent guilt
Made for a protagonist that mirrored her story

The teacher asked for comments
Little Girl said what she thought
Eyes pointed in her direction
All with the silence of a hawk watching its prey

"Oh, Honey"
Little Girl tensed
The voice the teacher used was guilty
"That girl has anorexia"

It was as if the world was backwards
Then, jolted into the right direction
Little Girl's mind went for a tailspin

Little Girl knew she didn't have an eating disorder
Those were for pretty skinny girls
Who glided across the earth
Ethereal angels

She was not skinny
There were the rolls she had when she sat down
The way her fingers didn't go around her arm
The way her hair started to fall out...

Oh No

Is she less of a little girl
Than she thought?

It Changes

The world is shifting
Into a flashing arrow
Pointing at Little Girl
Indicating what's wrong

She wishes to run away
So she does
Going to the bathroom
Purging it all up

There is no easy way
To be confronted by yourself
To know that there is something wrong
That you cannot fix it if you tried

Voices rambling inside her head
Screaming
YOU NEED HELP
YOU NEED TO DIE
STOP

That last one was her own
And then sitting on the bathroom floor

Mirroring so many painful nights
She knows that she can finally
Finally
Be
More

She can be herself
The girl who she hasn't been since
First Fucking Grade

She can learn to call herself
Her own name
Her only name
Once again

(There is a joy in names, a glimmer, a recognition,
    but only if you are the name that you can
    become. Esperanza is hope and she can be
    whoever she wants to be. <u>She can be herself.</u>)

For a Name

A name is the container
Of the dreams that preceded it
Esperanza is hope
For a lost marriage
For a lost child

When Esperanza became Estie
After the divorce
It meant to not have a father
To leave one half of herself behind

And then she morphed

Into someone not like herself
Someone named Little Girl
Who craved to be anyone else

Who saw other little girls
Getting praise from their mothers
With confidence that illuminated
From their glittery shoes
And smiles that seemed real

And so she forgot her name
While she was trekking through the jungle
Of her own (un)worthiness
Until she remembered

Esperanza can contain
The hope she has for *herself*
And that changes everything

Confrontations with Cold Mothers (Part I)

Every daughter has a fear
A primal instinct
The feel of their Mothers' wrath

Fathers have flames
That spark a wildfire
But you turn into Little Girl again
And he'll calm down

But mothers know
That Little Girl doesn't exist

That you are always you
No matter what
They see you for who you are
Not the mastermind you pretend to be

If fires are fathers
Mothers are tsunamis
Because how do you stop a tsunami?
You can't
The destruction lasts forever

Confrontations with Cold Mothers (Part II)

Esperanza knows a flood is coming
One that rivals Noah's Ark
This one is also
Marked by the decline of humanity

She opens the door of her house
And is drowned by the silence of falsehoods
Of a guilty Mother
Who was never expecting a daughter
(Never wanted one)

They stand there
Quietly calculating the distance between them
It is as if they were on opposite sides of the Pacific

Mother knows
Like all Mothers know
That her now grown up girl needs some help
And it's as if the water full of ignorance of
    each other

Washes away

You know what this means right?
Yes, Esperanza nods

It means
Doctors
Therapists
Confusion
Revelations

It means that her life might *finally* begin

Scales of Decay

There's a doctor's appointment
Willing, waiting
For a girl with a body
Two sizes too small

They greet Little Girl
She corrects them (it's Esperanza now)
And is led like a lamb
To be shown and faulted for her own body

But there's a difference now
In this time then the others
There are no pocket weights
Not this time

This time it's revealed she's severely underweight
How she can't do a sit up
How she is *weak*

And then they say
Poor Little Girl
Who has money and not much else

Esperanza sees the sadness in their eyes
The pity seeping into her smock-covered body

But all she can think about
Is the gnawing ache
That bites at her on the way home

When she throws the ED clinic pamphlets
Scattering across her room
The ache turns into rage

There is no thought of BMI or anorexia (her
    apparent condition)
Or clinics on the other side of the country

There is only the thought that she isn't a Little Girl
She can let herself grow

Aphenphosmphobia

(noun)

Definition (scientifically): fear of being touched

Definition (Esperanza): the closest she can find for
   a fear of meaningful

Connection

~~A fear of family~~

It started when Mother said

That her stepmother

Was influencing her too much

And her father was in on her scheme

The same stepmother

Who bought her pretty dresses

And called her once a month

To say hi

To let her know there was someone who cared

(Sometimes she answered; sometimes she didn't.

   She always knew when it was her.)

Or maybe it started

When Mother started resenting her

For her undeniable youth
The undeniable privilege she possessed

Esperanza knew who Mother was
A bitch with good intentions
Who wanted to crawl out of her dirtbag city
And didn't expect a daughter to be part of
    the package

Now it seems that Mother's fog has cleared
Rolled away with the rude awakening
Of her daughters eating disorder
Of her own disordered eating

She reaches out by herself
First with Paris
Then with her research

Esperanza catches her
When passing Mother's bedroom
She sees papers and books scattered
All with handwritten notes

They talk about resentment
They talk about reconnection

Then there are the little things
How Mother says I love you
Her good nights resonating through the
    apartment
How one night she crawls into Esperanza's
    bedroom and says
I am a terrible mother
And *I am so so sorry*
And *I was selfish*
How Esperanza says *I know*

They stare at each other
Experiencing that everlasting mother-daughter
    bond for the first time

And then Mother
Snaps out of her own glory
And realizes
How her hands seem to be wanting for touch
How Esperanza's hands might be ready to feel it

Mothers aren't perfect
But sometimes they can change
And for Esperanza?

That's enough

Almost Alive

It's been two weeks
Esperanza feels almost alive again
Mother knows what to do
Send her back to school

It's been two weeks
And Esperanza is dreading education
She knows she'll have to become Little Girl

Once again

It's been two weeks
She's done some contemplating
About who she has been
Who she wants to be

She knows what she was
A bully, a bitch
Who was so afraid of her own shadow
That she made other's disappear

Then the problem of her bestest friend
Who was never really her friend at all

Miss Hot Pink (her name is Kallista, she
    remembers)
She remembers a lot about Kallista
More than she would like

She remembers the weighing
The gaslighting
The names that were taken away from her

Most of all she remembers the fear
Of not having a pack
Girls to go to the bathroom with
Targeting others behind their backs

But for every good memory
Of the hints of dopamine Kallista gave out
    like candy
She knows that what Kallista really saw in her
Are her insecurities

Esperanza is stronger now

Her iPhone weighs in her pocket
Like a gun in a soldiers hand
She whips it out with precision

Texts *I don't want to be your friend anymore. I hope
      you understand.*
Presses send

(Sometimes it hurts more to hold onto someone
      than to let them go)

(Sometimes the phantom weight of a burden
      lifts, and you were so crushed by it that now
      you can fly)

Esperanza has found her wings
And she intends to use them

An interlude:
the insecure girl
formerly known as
Miss Hot Pink

There is a girl
Who grew up too fast
And was taught that lying
Was how to get ahead

She has a sister
Had a sister
(She ran away when Kallista was six)
Left a note saying
Get out when you can

The sister was never found
And Kallista learned
That you didn't have to run away from
    your problems
In order to solve them

You just needed to blend in

She crafted her persona
From the bottom up
Starting when her mom's wealthy cousin
Came to their house
And had a sneer on her face the entire time

Kallista knew what she saw
The one bedroom apartment
Flea bitten couches
A stack of three-day-old dishes

It isn't much her Mother said
But it's ours

She knew better
Her scholarship (fully paid) knew it, too
So she lied about a house in the Hamptons
Befriended the wealthiest kids in her class
And made sure to take from them
Whatever she could get

And so when she convinced another Little Girl
That she was Miss Hot Pink, not Kallista
She felt herself running away
From the home that she's ashamed to live in

Until there is no other self
Only her, only wealth
Yet she hugs her mother every morning
And doesn't let anyone come to her house

(The thing about lies? They all come out eventually
And Kallista's starts
Pouring out with a text.)

Reckoning

Before we continue
With our one-sided tale
Remember that Mean Girls are still little girls
Cut them and their secrets some slack

Esperanza was always a terrible liar
Except when the truth would save her
She supposed Kallista was the same way

When she sent that text
She didn't expect an answer back
Merely to be blocked or ghosted
(It's not like they'll be close after this)

Instead she gained a text
As long as the river of tears she shed over Kallista
Where every word felt like a punch in the gut

You don't even know the pain I've gone through
The opening statement
How much I've done for you
How much I've worked for what I had

Esperanza knows that Kallista's life is a lie

And she took the bait

How many times has she complained about
    poor people?

How many times did Esperanza agree?

Ashamed, angry, awestruck

Esperanza is a Little Girl once more

Who only wants feelings

That other people gave her

Back to School

It's been fourteen days without binging or purging
Mother's made sure of it
But in school there is no supervision
The tension sits, rotting

She lost trust with herself
Long ago
The first time she said she'd quit
And went back the next day

This time though there's a reason
She needs to be human again
It will mean sucking up the pride
She has always been given

She is was a mean Little Girl
Alienating those who don't have power
Rejecting those who weren't enough for her
Simpering with those who promised they were

There's still that spark of arrogance
That says she's a queen
Bowing down to peasants

That makes her newfound smile

Seem a little fake
And pushes kids away

The Only Queen
in Her Castle

Each day is a struggle
For friendship, for acknowledgement
Laughter that was once given so easily
Is now held back
Because of her

If Kallista could be the villain in her story
Then Esperanza could be one to another
The poor little rich girl
With everything except a dad
Beauty, brains, and boys
It made others outlandishly jealous

There were the other things too
How she laughed when others were down
With teachers who seemed to favor her

So yes they've seen the tension between her and
    her so called friend
(They all knew that Kallista has hated her for years)
It's all anyone can talk about at their tables

They see those desperate smiles
How she's practically begging for a friend
But they think it's not my problem
So Esperanza's left alone
Like she has been since the beginning

Breaking

Esperanza is tears and anger
As she steps through the front door of her home
Brittle hair almost breaking
At the sound of her voice

One can only be nice for so long
Until cracks start to show
Breaking until the order has changed

She feels Little Girl taking over
With her lies that mean a lot
And so she states Kallista is a bully
Without feeling it true to herself

I need to transfer
I need to get out of here
There's no need for me to be in this place
    any longer

Mother listens
Dad does too
For his little girl is hurt

And he's ridden with guilt for not being there
   to kiss her
Wouldn't you?

Esperanza is getting her new start
Where she can finally have her name be hers

Yet creeping out
In the not so nice parts of her mind
They say a new school
Is where you can be a Queen

Welcome to the Theater

We open on the scene in progress. Esperanza is alone, waiting. Someone from the past is alone, looking. The first needs a friend, the second is a teenage girl.

Odette: Can I sit here?
Esperanza: Go ahead.

They pause, waiting for the other to speak. An awkward silence, then—

Odette: So I hear you're going by Esperanza now?
Esperanza: Well, it is my name.

Another silence. Esperanza notes that Odette is skinnier than she was when they played their games an infinity ago. She hates herself for noticing.

Odette: It's kind of crazy you aren't sitting next to Kallista. I mean, you guys were always together. Rumors are everywhere, you know?

Esperanza blinks, she didn't know anyone else knew her name. Immediately that sense of importance washes away. The emptiness shows on her face.

Odette: Anyways, I just wanted to say that most of the grade is on your side, I mean she always gossiped about you and said she hated you and all that stuff. No one really believed her, but I mean what are you gonna do, y'know?

Anyways, I just thought that you should know all that because my mom says it's better to know the truth than to hear sweet lies. I'll see you around, okay?

The emptiness contorts into confusion then horror. She feels tears in her eyes and bile in her throat. Ashamed that this nobody who she once bullied in lower school became the one who pitied her. And jealous because she doesn't feel Odette is a nobody at all. Because she wants Odette to stay and keep telling her brutal truths and to say I forgive you. She wants to be a bystander in her own story.

Esperanza: Um yeah, see you around.

But that's not an option, her two choices are this. To run to the bathroom and stick a finger down her throat in order to vent in the only way she knows how or to run to the guidance counselor's room and say what Odette told her. She chooses the latter. The door is locked.

Double-Sided Dread

Deleted is the Instagram bio
That says her school's name of the past
Now introducing the new one
Nobody blinked

Esperanza wouldn't be lying
If she said she wished for a commotion
A storm of people saying why they wish for
    her to stay

Instead
Nothing
Even the constant refreshing wouldn't do
It's seems that she's as gone from
    everyone's hearts
As she is from her past
Yet there's still hope
That those once best friends
Will come back to her
Make it all like before
(She forgot that she was miserable)

So while Mother praises
The alumni of the school she'll soon attend
So while Father praises
The half-sister who is making friends

There is a palpable loss
A journey now ended

She looks back
At the brick building
Built before women got the right to vote
Intrusive thoughts flood through her
C'est la vie

A Work in Context

Esperanza's been wallowing for days
There's just nothing to do now she's
   reforming herself
No camp, no friends
Just a long stretch

Until one day
Mother can't bear it
Seeing her daughter behave
Like the unluckiest person alive

Sure, she's had some bad luck
But can't she see how grateful she should be?
How spoiled she is
Bigger pictures would die for her life
And now she's wasting away

It makes her think of past friends
The uncomfortable looks they shared
When they Googled her family

There's always a voice

In the back of her head
Saying, *You'd never be here without them*
Another voice says
You're right

But Esperanza wants to be alone
So she swallows her guilt
And sleeps

Crimson Streaks

It happens on Labor Day weekend
A ball of pain at the bottom of her stomach
Calling out for womanhood
To be given relief

Spilling everywhere
Esperanza knows what this means
That she is recovered, in remission
She could be considered healthy now

Healthy
What mothers say when their kid is slightly
    overweight
Perfectly healthy, it's just the sports
Body inclusive Instagram accounts
Sporting rolls saying that BMIs don't matter
You're doing just fine

She'd always scoff at their posts
It's just cheating
To compensate for their size
But now she can be considered one of them

Healthy
The word compresses on her tongue

She wants to swallow it whole
Like the mints she chewed frantically
Wants it to burn in her stomach
And never return

There's a flashback to the old days
When people's eyes would be in shock at the sight
    of her skin
Those bony arms
Encompassing her ribs

But still
Womanhood is wondrous, right?
For now she is healthy, fine, okay really
She can be healthy, maybe
She can fit into her size

Fever Breaks

There's a moment when everything gets better
The entirety of the self-help business is built on it
It is what Mother calls
A breaking fever
When you know everything will be alright

For Esperanza it is when she is in school
It's been two months since she's last purged
Mother is proud

The stubborn sun is still staying
In those early days of October
When it seems that the remnants of summer
Will last a lifetime
And the East Coast will never see snow again

For Esperanza it is when she feels excited for lunch
Because her new friends have saved her a spot
And the food is delicious
(She calls everyone there by their names)

And yes, she still doubts everyone
Hesitates to sit, to make a sound

Still glances at others unlike her
Or at the bathroom and wonders
Should I do it again?

But then Mother texts her
What do you want for dinner?
Which is another way of saying *I love you*
And she's squished in the middle of the lunchroom
Singing along to songs from 2010
Offkey tones hum around her
Her friend takes a picture of the joy on her face

So, yes
Everyone can exhale yet again
For they know
The fever is broken

Life Ain't a Fairytale

Esperanza is happy now, don't worry
She doesn't have to worry about college tuition
Or her parents' acceptance

Just whether she'll keep her grades up
Or make swim team captain

She knows, though
In sharing her story
There are still so many that cannot be her
Who cannot live the fairytale
That was her nightmare
For that, she apologizes

So many little girls
Dream of a climax
An epic showdown of sorts
But that rarely happens

Instead the triumphs and tribulations
Continue over and over
In flowery prose

Until the reader wants to drop it
It's the same thing over and over

Life is a series of events
That continues in a circle
Eat, sleep, talk, drink
Try not to die

A melancholic story
That you ponder in the shower

There are instead:
Dreams of conversations
Smiles
The feeling of being known
For you are known to the world

(Don't forget it)

Your life is an epic poem
As is Esperanza's
As is mine
We all end up stuck in our own plots
But you decided to read another
And for that, I thank you

So do me a favor

Before you go

And eat a cupcake

Before the cupcake eats you

Acknowledgements

THANK YOU TO MY publishing team for their support. To my parents, Erica and Geraldo Rivera, who encouraged me in every way possible. What an incredible journey it has been! To Alex Davis, the first proofreader and reviewer on Goodreads, there is a reason you are my soul sister. I look forward to more time together. To my Aunt Marjorie, who got me through the toughest times. And lastly, to my strong, brave, beautiful readers—I hope that you will find the Esperanza in you, no matter how hard it may seem.